Hannah's Happy Dog Tales

Rescued!

Written by Coleen Balch

Illustrated by Cathleen Berry

Grindstone
Press

NOTICE TO THE READER

Published by Grindstone Press
www.GrindstonePress.com

Printed in the United States of America

Contents

DEDICATION

We dedicate the *Hannah's Happy Dog Tales* series, and are ourselves dedicated, to pit bulls everywhere who have endured abandonment, exploitation, neglect, and cruelty on all levels. It is beyond shame that they bear such brutality in a nation so blessed. It is heart-rending that so many Americans fail to see the treatment many of these dogs experience as unacceptable or fail to understand the true nature of pit bulls. Once America's dog, many now are feared or fought, and they suffer the consequences on a daily basis. It is to those animals we dedicate this series, *Hannah's Happy Dog Tales*, with the sincere hope that all pit bulls may have only happy tales.

We sincerely thank members of our military for their service. Freedom isn't free, and we are grateful for all of your sacrifices. It is to you and your families all around the world, that we dedicate this first volume of the *Hannah's Happy Dog Tales* series.

ACKNOWLEDGMENTS

Our gratitude goes to the many folks who took time out of their schedules to help tell this tale. Your earnestness and dedication to our purpose is greatly appreciated. Thank you all.

To **Jeremy Bogan**, the inspiration for the character of the same name. The real Jeremy is an exceptional young man, worthy of all accolades due every American service member, and then some. He represents the strength, sincerity, and commitment of all our men and women in service to this nation. A genuine, kind, and compassionate human being, we are proud to know him and can only hope the fictional Jeremy does him justice in some small way;

To **Avery Page** for her patience and creativity in conveying shape and structure to the appearance of Priscilla;

To **Robert KarlesKent** for lending his kind expression to the countenance of the dog catcher;

To **Justin Turner** for sharing his likeness and representing hard-working EMTs everywhere;

To **David Balch** for representing his fellow veterans and supporting photo shoots with Hannah;

To **Nathan Balch** for his photography expertise;

To **Britta Berry**, **Wendy**, **Zach**, **Ethan**, and **Avery Page**, **Jaden Nelson**, **Jason Balch**, **Sabrina Paterniti**, **Cathy Wolf**, RN, BSN, MST, and **Ric Mitchell** for reviewing the manuscript as it progressed and for offering many astute insights;

And to **Hannah**, **Spuds**, **Liberty**, and **Nashota**—all very real pit bulls with very real rescue stories—just for being their lovable, huggable selves.

The Real Pit Bulls in the Story

HANNAH

Locked in a vacant house, Hannah was abandoned by her humans. By the time her mother was seen considering a jump from a second story window, Hannah, her mom, and her only surviving sibling were very weak. Despite it all, she is a docile, sweet girl who loves everyone. She happily embraces all the rescued pit bulls staying at Central New York Pitstop Rescue on their way to loving, forever homes like hers.

SPUDS

Spuds—the best introduction to the world of pit bulls anyone could have. He survived an abusive owner, life on the streets dragging a heavy chain, and being hit by a truck. Then no one would adopt him because he was a pit bull with a history. Despite it all, he loved people! There was never a more affectionate or grateful dog, or one with a greater spirit. He is the reason Central New York Pitstop Rescue was started.

LIBERTY

Liberty's first owner didn't want her or any of the other puppies. In fact, he paid so little attention to her mom, he didn't know she was pregnant until he discovered them at three days old. Then he threatened to "dispose" of them. His neighbor spoke up and alerted Central New York Pitstop Rescue, where adoptions were arranged for her siblings; but Liberty was a keeper. Always a puppy at heart, Liberty is a watcher. She doesn't miss much and keeps everyone's secrets!

NASHOTA

Nashota was found wondering the streets at about 4 months old. She had no tags and no one answered ads and posters searching for her humans. She received food and water and languished at a pound for 4 more months until her time was near. After moving to Central New York Pitstop Rescue, this bundle of energy found a perfect home with a loving dad, and has a great life that includes love and tags!

Introduction

The term "pit bull" is commonly used to refer to dogs with a certain appearance, rather than as a reference to a specific breed. In the 19th century British breeders linked bull dogs and terriers resulting in what we now know as the American Staffordshire Terrier, American Pit Bull Terrier, and Staffordshire Bull Terrier. They were used in bull and bear baiting and dog fighting in the 1800s. Once the darlings of early 20th century America as Petey of Spanky and Our Gang, the Buster Brown Shoes dog, and Sergeant Stubby (the several-times decorated hero of World War I), the image of the "pit bull" has deteriorated to one of viciousness, which has somehow made it acceptable to physically and mentally abuse these animals. Stories of dogfights for sport are well known. Commonly, when there has been a dog attack in the neighborhood, the media creates a pit bull story out of it. Backyard breeders have considerably added to the reputation of the pit bull as an aggressive dog that every macho bad boy should own.

The truth is far from one of crazed attacker. The actual breeds often referred to as pit bulls were bred specifically for non-aggression toward humans. Research has proven these dogs to have dispositions similar or superior to other breeds generally considered common family dogs, such as golden retrievers and poodles. And scientific studies have demonstrated that the bite of the pit bull is less than that of a German shepherd.

For reasons known only to the human aggressor, pit bulls are beaten, burned, exploited, starved, forced to fight, and abandoned every day in America. As appalling as this is, over the last few decades, people have come to believe the media propaganda and fear even the name or sight of a pit bull. This is not the American way. Pit bulls, like every other pet, just want to be loved. They will return that love a hundred times over. They want to live in a loving home with food, water, medical care, and affection that they will return with absolute devotion for life.

Help us put an end to the disgrace so many suffer and restore the pit bull to its rightful position as the affectionate, intelligent, obedient family pet they really are. No amount of compassion is too small, and it's never too late to show a pit bull the compassion they deserve.

Chapter One

"And in the weather tonight, more rainstorms expected. This may be the rainiest spring on record. There's already been two inches of rain today, and added to the four inches we've had this week, it may be a very wet weekend with possible flooding in the low areas along the river." The weatherman continued as Mr. Peevish turned his attention away from the TV and looked out the window.

"There they are again! I knew it," he gasped. "Those four pit bulls are running everywhere in this town. Someone has to stop them. I'm calling the dogcatcher again right now."

"Yes, Mr. Peevish, I know about the dogs," sighed the dogcatcher. "But, really, there is no such thing as a pit bull. People use that term to mean dogs from as many as eighteen different breeds they mistakenly think look like a pit bull. Besides, they haven't done any harm."

"No harm? You must be kidding! These are dangerous dogs. You can't wait till they do harm. You have to catch them now!" Mr. Peevish was getting very red in the face.

"Mr. Peevish, please." said the dogcatcher. "There is no proof that pit bulls are any more dangerous than any other dog. They have to be trained to be mean. They aren't born that way!" The dogcatcher had brought many dogs back to the pound over the years, but he always felt less worried about the pit bulls biting than most of the other breeds. "Saying all pit bulls are dangerous makes as much sense as saying all ice cream is chocolate."

But Mr. Peevish wasn't giving up. "I don't care what you say, I want them caught!" he bellowed.

"Oh, fine, I'll drive around to see if I can find them," the dogcatcher said half-heartedly.

"Well you just better find them and take them to the pound, or I'll call the mayor!" Mr. Peevish was always calling the mayor and complaining about things he didn't like.

"Oh, Hannah, slow down, I'm getting all muddy running so fast!" cried Nashota. Hannah was the leader of the group. Nashota was very young, still a puppy really, and even though she loved to play and run and chase her tail, she did not like to be wet, especially from muddy water. She was still small for her age, and she was always hungry, but there was never enough food to fill up her tummy. She didn't remember much about her life before she met Hannah. She remembered a mom and other puppies all in a big basket. One after another, people would come and pay money and take them away.

But no one came to take her. One day, the man who had been taking the money and giving away the puppies picked up Nashota and put her in the back seat of his car. After awhile, the car stopped and the man picked her up, dropped her on the side of the road, and drove away. If Hannah hadn't been in the shadows where it happened, Nashota might have been in big trouble. Hannah stepped out of her hiding place just in time to stop Nashota from walking out in front of a car. Then she showed Nashota how to find food and water, even though there was never enough to eat. Still, Hannah became like a mother to Nashota, helping her grow up

and be safe. Nashota was very grateful for Hannah.

Spuds was bigger and much older. He had learned how to survive on the streets by swiping food and ducking trouble. He turned around and snarled at Nashota. "Don't you worry about being wet and muddy. Worry about finding a dry place to sleep tonight. That'll never happen if you keep slowing us down." Spuds just wanted to eat and settle in for a good night's rest. Well, what he really wanted was a nice forever-home with a warm blanket and a bowl of food every day. But he especially wanted someone to care about him, someone he could snuggle up next to and watch TV with in the evening and go for a walk in the park with on sunny days. He wanted the love of a human being, and if he had that, he would love the person back and take care of him, too. He had a home once. Well, it wasn't much of a home, really. He ran away because it wasn't safe for him in that home. Eventually, he met Hannah, and from then on, they took care of each other.

Liberty laughed and dashed at Nashota, knocking her into a puddle on purpose. "Oh come, on, let's play in the rain. It's so much fun," she giggled. "Yuck," cried Nashota. Spuds groaned.

Even though she was two years old last autumn, Liberty was a puppy that never seemed to grow up. To her, it was always playtime. However, being on the street with no human to care for her meant not having regular meals or toys like the pull-ropes and balls she loved so

4

much. So she tried to create games like splashing in puddles to keep from thinking about how empty her tummy was. Liberty had been one of dozens of puppies where she was born, all of different breeds. Her home was a little cage with her brothers and sisters. There were many little cages with many dogs all around her. They never got out to play and usually had little to eat. One night the humans at that place took Liberty and her brothers and sisters to a dark ally and left them there. They didn't have their mom with them and didn't know what to do. Liberty struck out on her

own and found lots of humans who thought she was so cute and would occasionally give her food, but nobody would take her home with them. Liberty longed for a real home, even though she really didn't know what a home was. When she met Hannah, she was very hungry and scared. Hannah helped her find something to eat and told her wonderful stories about what a nice home they would have together one day. The stories helped Liberty sleep.

Hannah knew she had to work hard to keep her pals together and moving. She was always alert for dangers like the dogcatcher and had to lead her pals to a safe place out of the rain, where they could sleep and maybe find some food. Hannah had a real home once. She barely remembered it, though. It was a long time ago. She had a boy who played ball with her and gave her puppy cookies. One day, a big truck came to her home and loaded all the furniture in the house on it. The boy and his parents got in the car and drove away. They didn't take

Hannah for the ride, and they never came back. The house was empty and cold, and there was no food in her bowl. She didn't know why she was left behind, and it made her very sad to be so lonely. She knew she had to try to find her boy, but with no idea where they all went, Hannah wandered for days and weeks and months without ever finding them.

She liked her friends, though. It was a little like having a family again to be with Spuds, Liberty, and Nashota. But she still longed for a warm forever-home with a human to love her. It was tough being out on the run, but no one wanted them. No one would take care of them and feed them or play with them. And she knew all of them needed baths badly. Of course, she didn't say that to them. Nashota would never let anyone give her a bath, and Liberty just wanted to pounce and splash in mud all the time.

Sergeant Jeremy had just come home from Afghanistan. He was in the Army over there until just last week. For almost two years, he worked with other soldiers who tried to bring peace to the Middle Eastern country. The sergeant had made many friends there. He could still talk with them sometimes on the computer, but adjusting to being without them was hard. He smiled to himself when he realized it was a lot like the last day of school growing up, when he was glad he could stay home all summer, but it meant not seeing many of his friends for what seemed like forever. Now Sergeant Jeremy was home. He knew he could be in the Army reserves or maybe stay in the service doing a job in America. He had to decide. Still, as he was driving along Main Street, his thoughts went back to the people he left behind. He would really miss his friends back there. He knew he had to focus on fixing up his new house in the country and starting a new job, but he was feeling very lonely.

All along Main Street, the rain was creating big puddles. At times, it rained so hard that Sergeant Jeremy could barely see through the windshield. Suddenly, there was a loud cracking sound, and a huge tree limb came crashing down just as the sergeant's car passed under the tree. The limb was very heavy, and it landed on his roof. He tried to hold on, but it sent his car out of control, crashing into a telephone pole. The car hit with so much force that the doors flew wide open. Jeremy was tossed around like a rag doll, even though he had his seatbelt snuggly in place. He hit his head so hard that he lost consciousness, and there was a trickle of blood dripping down his face from his forehead. His right leg was jammed under the dashboard. He needed help, but no one was there to help him.

Hannah stopped running, and all her pals stopped, too. They saw what had happened as they were about to run across the street. "That man is in danger," she said to the others.

"Someone will come and help him. People always help people, even though they won't help us dogs," Spuds grumbled. "Let's just go before someone tries to catch us."

"No, Spuds, we have to help him. There's no one around, and by the time someone calls the ambulance, it may be too late," Hannah answered.

"But what can we do? We're only dogs!" Liberty and Nashota declared in unison.

"We can do plenty. Follow me!" Hannah called as she raced to the rescue. The others followed, but they were very worried about this idea of helping a human. "Spuds, you have the strongest jaw. Bite through the man's seatbelt so we can pull him out," Hannah directed. "If we don't hurry, another car could come by and hit this one. Then there will be two cars and more people to worry about!" Spuds paused only a moment, and then he went to work chewing through the tough seat belt that held Sergeant Jeremy in his seat. "Nashota, hurry, you're the smallest. Get in under the dashboard and free his leg so we can pull him out!" Hannah was barking out orders like a sergeant now! Nashota never hesitated. She wiggled up underneath and worked Jeremy's leg loose quickly. "Liberty, you're the strongest. We'll need

that strength if we are going to get the man out. Get ready to pull him from the front seat on my signal." By then, Spuds had completely chewed through the seatbelt. All that remained was a good heave-ho, and they would have Sergeant Jeremy out of the car. Hannah looked up and down the street for human help and to be sure no cars were coming that might hit them. She announced it was safe, so Liberty took hold of Jeremy's jacket collar, and Spuds and Hannah grabbed other parts of

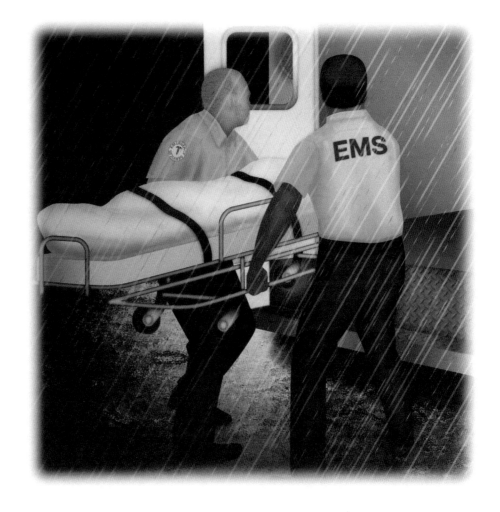

his jacket. With their powerful jaws they gave a great tug and freed him from the car. They pulled him over to the side of the road where he would be safe until another human came to help. Of course, Mr. Peevish, who lived just a short distance up the road, heard the accident happen and called 911. Now the dogs could hear the sirens coming.

"OK, everybody, let's get out of here," Hannah called. But Nashota was too busy licking the man's face, wishing he would wake up and pet her. She didn't move until the ambulance pulled to a stop. In the rainy shadows of the night, the ambulance crew could see the four pit bulls as they backed away from the emergency scene.

"Hey, Charlie, did you see that? Those dogs were pulling this guy out of the car! Have you ever seen such a thing before?" one medic hollered to the other as they rushed to the sergeant's side.

"Yeah, Justin," the other said. "That's pretty amazing. They should get an award for bravery!" Very quickly they braced his leg and lifted him onto the stretcher. In just a few minutes they had Sergeant Jeremy in the ambulance and on the way to the hospital.

Mr. Peevish ambled to the kitchen and fixed himself a little supper. Then he returned to his TV, which, by now, was blaring a breaking news story about the amazing rescue. The medics from the ambulance were being interviewed about the pit bulls they saw saving the sergeant's life. The reporter asked what happened to the dogs, but no one seemed to know. Mr. Peevish knew. He saw the dogcatcher's van pulling away right after the ambulance. "Thank goodness those dogs won't be a problem around here anymore," he sneered.

Chapter Two

"Sergeant Jeremy, you're a lucky fellow!" the emergency room doctor said. You got out of this accident with a mild concussion, a couple stitches, and a broken leg. It could have been much worse!"

The sergeant tried to smile, but it hurt too much.

Sergeant Jeremy's nurse was standing next to him. She had talked to the medics who brought him in. "Sergeant that was amazing. Do you know those dogs that saved your life tonight? Are they yours? The story is all over the news!"

"No, I pretty much don't remember anything. What is the news saying about it?" he asked, changing position on the stretcher and grimacing from the pain in his leg.

"Well, a man who lives near the place of your accident said four pit bulls were running around there when that limb fell on your car. It made you spin out of control and crash into something. The medics who responded said the dogs pulled you out of the car and away from danger. They're real heroes. But someone called the dogcatcher, and now they're all at the pound. No telling what will happen to the dogs now," the nurse reported. She turned the sergeant's TV on to the news, so he could watch the account of the accident.

One reporter went to the pound and interviewed the dogcatcher. They even let the reporter get pictures of the four dogs. Jeremy studied the dogs on the TV screen carefully. He thought they looked scared and a little thin. He found himself wanting to hug each one and give them a bone and a proper home. But how could he adopt four dogs all at once? He had a nice back yard at his new house. They would like that. And he would like coming home after work at night to the happy greetings of those four furry faces and wagging tails. He could get a big couch for his new house, and they could all sit and watch dog shows on TV at night. But first he would feed them delicious meals and give them all treats. What a life for all of them! What a change for all of them!

His pain medicine was finally starting to work, and it was making him very sleepy, but before he dozed off, he made his decision. "You're right! I have to find those dogs and help them. They risked their lives to save mine." Sergeant Jeremy was thinking about his army buddies and how everyone always helped each other. "This is no different; I have to save *them* now." He wanted to get up and get started on this rescue of his own, but his nurse gently reminded him that he needed to rest and build his strength.

"You need to start healing that leg, Sergeant. I'll call the dog pound and make sure the dogs will be kept safe until you can get there." She had adopted her own dog from the pound, and she was sure it would be a safe place for the four heroes to wait a few days for their new home.

The next day, the doctor said the sergeant could go home as soon as he learned to walk with crutches. Jeremy was a good student and learned quickly to maneuver on them. "Sergeant, be careful. You may not feel well for a few days," the doctor reminded him.

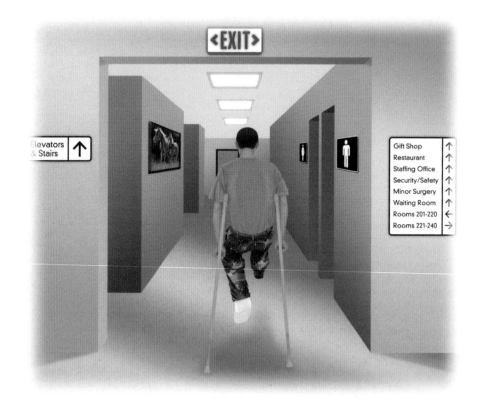

But Sergeant Jeremy felt very well. He was determined to take his rescuers home. The first thing he did was get a ride to the pound. He was very excited when he arrived and met the dogcatcher. The man seemed kind and cared about how the dogs were doing and what would happen to them. But the sergeant was very sad when he learned that he couldn't adopt the pit bulls because he didn't have a fence around his yard.

"Young man, we would love to let you adopt these dogs. They deserve a good home, and I think you would take excellent care of them. But those dogs have made some of the townspeople upset because they run all over. They tip over garbage cans looking for food scraps and scare drivers when they run across roads. We can't let them go anywhere without a way to confine them. They have to be safe, and so do the people who live around here. People think they are a real menace and even dangerous," explained the dogcatcher.

Sergeant Jeremy's smile went away. "Those dogs are not a danger to the people who live around here. Everyone should be happy about these dogs. If not for them, I might not be here! I bet they've helped out in lots of places." Try as he may, Jeremy could not change the dogcatcher's mind.

"Jeremy, the mayor doesn't like to hear about unhappy people in his town, especially during an election year. If I let those pit bulls go without a safe way to control them, I could lose my job," he explained.

Sergeant Jeremy knew there wouldn't be much time to figure out what to do. He had a nice little house with a nice little yard. It had big trees for shade on a hot sunny day that would

be perfect for the dogs. He could throw sticks and frisbees for them to chase and bring back. There was plenty of space for the dogs to run and get exercise. Those were all things that would make the dogcatcher happy. But it didn't have a fence around it.

Fences are very expensive, and the sergeant didn't have much money. He could afford to pay the dogs' fees to get them out of the pound, but that wasn't enough. The dogcatcher was right. The dogs needed to be safe. And the neighbors wouldn't like the dogs running around, no matter whose dogs they were. But without enough money to build a fence, Jeremy couldn't help them, not even one of them.

Hannah and her pals were in kennels behind a partially closed door. Jeremy couldn't see them, but they were watching him. "Sergeant Jeremy sure looks awful," whispered Hannah.

"He would look a whole lot worse if we hadn't pulled him out of that car wreck last night," quipped Nashota.

"No, Nashota, Hannah means he looks awfully sad. I think he really wants to get us out of here," Spuds clarified.

"Maybe he will," added Liberty hopefully. "Maybe he'll take us home with him and let us play in his back yard. Do you think he has a rope we can pull on? I love to play tug-o-war."

"Oh, for goodness sake, Liberty, he doesn't have a rope. You heard the dogcatcher. The sergeant doesn't even have a fence, and pit bulls in a yard without a fence is not something this town will ever let happen," grumbled Spuds. "Besides, it's not so bad here. It's warm and dry, and they feed us every day."

Sergeant Jeremy was still trying to convince the dogcatcher to let him adopt all four pit bulls. "You know, when I was in the Army, soldiers didn't treat each other this way. If a soldier saved your life, you didn't just walk away. You were grateful and always looked for ways to pay him back. I want to pay these dogs back. They saved my life!" argued Jeremy.

"I know, son. I understand how you feel, and I am so glad you want to help them. So many people don't understand these dogs or just don't care." Jeremy thought he detected a little sadness in the dogcatcher's voice. "But there's no sense in rushing into this. Let's try to come up with a good solution—one that works for you, the dogs, and the neighbors. Let's think about this a while. You let me know if you come up with a good idea, and I'll let you know if I do." Now Jeremy thought he heard hope in the dogcatcher's voice. Or was it just that he wanted to hear hopefulness? The dogcatcher really liked Sergeant Jeremy. And secretly, he really liked those four pit bulls, even if they did make his job difficult.

"How are you going to get home Jeremy? You don't have a car anymore, and you certainly can't walk there. Come on, I have to go out toward your end of town. I'll give you a ride. I just got my old convertible out of storage, and I'd love to put the top down on this sunny spring afternoon."

Jeremy thanked the dogcatcher for his kindness. "I appreciate your help, and thank you for taking good care of the dogs."

"You're welcome, young man." The dogcatcher winked at Jeremy. "You go ahead on out to the car. It'll take you a couple minutes to get there on that bad leg, and I have something to do out back. It'll just take me a minute."

As Jeremy began to pick his way out on his crutches, the dogcatcher slipped out to the kennel area where the dogs were. As he opened the door he could see four sad faces and droopy tails. "Now stop that, all of you," he commanded. "My head may be gray, but I have a few tricks up my sleeves. I have a lot of friends. I think we just need to talk to some of them and see what happens when we all put our old heads together." The dogs weren't sure what he was going to do, but it sounded hopeful so they agreed to keep their tails high!

It was a sunny day, and the warmth of the spring sun made Jeremy feel better as he rode along in the dogcatcher's convertible. The breeze felt good in his hair, and he remembered how happy he was to be back home in the United States again. It wasn't long before the

dogcatcher pulled the big convertible into the sergeant's driveway. Jeremy climbed out and steadied himself on his crutches as he waved good-bye to the dogcatcher. As he struggled to get up the sidewalk and front steps, he had no idea where the dogcatcher was going next. He didn't see the convertible turn into the parking lot of the home improvement store, and he didn't see the dogcatcher talking to his friend, the owner of the store, as they walked through the fencing department.

The next day, Sergeant Jeremy had a very big surprise. A delivery truck pulled up to the curb, two men got out, and they began unloading equipment, supplies, and fencing materials. "Hello!" they called to Jeremy as he hopped and stumbled out the front door with a look of disbelief on his face.

"Stop!" Jeremy called to them. "Stop! I didn't order all this. I can't pay for this. There's been a big mistake!"

"Are you Sergeant Jeremy?" asked one of the workers.

"Well, yes, but . . ."

"Well, then, sir, there's no mistake. We'll just put all this around on the side of the house here, and the men who are coming to put it up will be here in a few minutes to get started. Have a good day," the man said as he walked away.

"But wait, I can't pay for this. You have to take it back!" cried Jeremy.

"This invoice here," the man hollered, "says paid in full. I guess it's a gift. Hope you enjoy it!" As the men finished unloading the wood, another van arrived and out hopped four men who quickly went to work putting the fence up all around the sergeant's yard. It was beautiful.

Jeremy called the fence store, but they said they couldn't tell him anything because the fence was paid for in cash, and the buyer didn't leave his name. Jeremy had a tear in his eye. He knew what to do next. He had to get to the kennels where the four pit bulls were waiting.

The fence made it a perfect place for the four heroic pit bulls to live safely. The dogcatcher acted as though he had no idea about the surprise fence. "Sergeant, I don't know how you did it," he said with a smile, "but I am happy to tell you that you now meet the criteria, and you may adopt the dogs that saved your life! Let's take them all to your house now." The dogcatcher helped Jeremy up into the front seat, then walked all the dogs out to his van and put them in the back one last time. Only this time, the van ride was to a perfect forever-home. He winked at the pit bulls, and as he closed the van door, he whispered to them, "Didn't I tell you to keep your tails high?"

"Wow!" exclaimed Nashota. "Can you believe this? Look at the green grass all around us!" She started chasing her tail in circles all over the yard.

"This is beautiful!" Liberty agreed. "There's so much space to run around in. I can run for hours! And look here. We have a really long rope, so we can play tug-o-war! Come on, Spuds, grab the other end. See if you can pull me off my feet!"

"Not now," sighed Spuds. "I have to check the perimeter. I need to know if this fence is secure. We don't ever want to worry about Mr. Peevish or the dogcatcher getting in here." He trotted all the way around the yard examining every foot of the fence. There was one place where a couple of the fence boards were cracked down at ground level. It looked pretty safe as long as no one knew about it. Still, he decided to tell only Hannah. If the two younger dogs knew, they might make a game of trying to break the fence there, and that would be very bad.

Hannah chuckled. "Don't worry so much, Spuds, no one will ever see it. We are very lucky dogs. Look at this. Sergeant Jeremy got us each our very own food dishes and our very own bones. I love chewing on a bone. Each of us has a handsome new collar with our name on it. And inside

the house I saw a big soft pillow in the middle of the floor where we can nap." Hannah could finally relax. She had a perfect forever-home and a man who loved her. She didn't have to worry all the time about taking care of the others. Now Jeremy did that for all of them.

"I love the sergeant's big TV," announced Nashota. "I want to watch all those animal shows I've heard about. I love Lassie!" She sat there thinking for a moment and then turned to Hannah. "I'm really glad you convinced us to help him that rainy night when he had his accident. He is such a nice man, and it sure is good to have a safe place where someone cares about us."

Liberty agreed. "Plus he gave us all these great toys, and there's a big shady tree and lots of yard to run around and roll in. Life here is going to be so much fun!"

Each day, Sergeant Jeremy's leg got better, and he was finally able to go to work. And every day, all through the spring and summer, when Jeremy came home from work, he would play with his dogs. They loved to run after frisbees and bring them back and run after them again and again. The sergeant would hug his dogs and scratch them behind their ears. Then he would fill all their dishes with the most delicious dog food. After dinner, they would find a good movie—about dogs—and relax on the big new couch together. Jeremy and each of his dogs thought, "ahh, this is the life."

Chapter Three

"**N**ow, Priscilla, listen carefully," said the big man. There were new neighbors moving in next door to the sergeant. The man was in a fancy suit that didn't look at all like what Sergeant Jeremy wore to work. The man wore a tie and had on shiny shoes. The little girl he was talking to was wearing a pink and white dress with lace and frills all around it. Her hair was in curls and ribbons. In her hand was one end of a leash. On the other end of the leash was a very little, very fluffy, very white dog.

Spuds was spying through a crack in the fence. He was always on patrol walking around the back yard, making sure all was secure. But, today there was a change in the routine. A new family was moving in next door, and Spuds didn't like this at all. He was worried about how the new neighbors would react to four pit bulls living next to them. What if they didn't like dogs? What if they called the dogcatcher? Not everyone understands pit bulls. Spuds had been around long enough to know that. And what if they didn't like Sergeant Jeremy?

"Oh, that's silly," he thought. "Who wouldn't like Sarge?" Then he called out to the rest of the gang, "looks like new neighbors moved into that house next door. Come listen to them."

They all came running with a steady stream of questions. "Do they have any dogs?" asked Nashota.

"Yeah, that like to play tug-o-war?" chattered Liberty.

"Do they seem nice?" inquired Hannah. She had finally been able to relax after all the time she had spent on the run. She didn't want to start worrying again.

The sun was low in the late afternoon sky, and four shadows were cast on the fence as all the dogs stood close to hear the conversation next door.

"Now Priscilla," repeated the man. "Listen carefully. We have a lovely new house and a lovely new yard. But it is surrounded by danger," warned the man. "On this side," he said as he swung his arm around to the right, "is a river. It's not a big river, but it is rocky, and with all the rain this spring, the water level is much higher than usual. Stay away from it at all times." He then swung his arm around to the left. "And on this side is a pack of terrible dogs. They are pit bulls, Priscilla, the most vicious and dangerous dogs there are. Why, I hate to think what they would do if they ever got hold of a pretty little girl like you. Just because there is a fence between them and us doesn't make them good to have around. Stay away from the fence, and stay away from those dogs!" the man cautioned.

The dogs looked at each other with dismay. It sounded like these would just be more people who didn't like pit bulls because they didn't understand them. "It isn't fair that people judge us before they even meet us," Hannah said sadly.

A lady came out of the house and repeated what the man said. "Yes, Priscilla, listen to your father, and never go near the dogs or the river." The lady was wearing a yellow dress, and her hair was up in a bun. Her skin was pale, like someone who rarely went out in the sunshine. "Be sure to hold on tightly to Winston," she told the girl. "You can walk him around the yard until supper is ready. The men haven't moved in all the furniture and boxes, so I don't know where Winston's toys are yet."

"Will you look at that dog!" exclaimed Spuds. "He has a collar that glitters. He's all fluffy and white. I bet he takes a bath every single day!"

"I bet that frilly little girl does, too," agreed Liberty. "Are you sure that thing is really a dog? I think it's one of those wind-up toys. No self-respecting dog would look like that!"

"Eww, baths! I hate getting wet," moaned Nashota.

Hannah was listening to all the chatter and thought it was time for her to say something. "Listen to yourselves. You are making judgments without meeting them, just like you said they are doing. It's no different, you know! Be nice to the girl and her dog. Maybe they will turn out to be fun to play with. And even if they don't, just remember how some people treat us just because they don't like how we look. That isn't fair, is it?" The others shook their heads. "Okay, then, let's wait and see what they are really like before we decide how we feel about them."

Well, they all agreed that they should give the new neighbors a chance before deciding if they were nice or not. But the next day they heard the little girl shouting, "Hey you stupid pit bulls. Locked up behind a fence, huh? That's just where you belong!"

A few days later Priscilla walked up to the fence and yelled, "My dog is better than any pit bull. He's fluffy and pretty, and you pit bulls are ugly."

Winston even got in on the act. He had a different way of talking that only Liberty could understand, but she translated for the other pit bulls. "Winston says we pit bulls are so lazy, that he bets he could run to the end of the fence in half the time we could." Then Winston ran up and down the length of the yard yipping and yapping, trying to show off.

Spuds couldn't understand anything that little dog yelped. "How come you understand him?" Spuds asked Liberty.

"Oh, it's simple, Spuds," Liberty responded. "Where I was born, there were dozens of other puppies all around. We were all in cages so we couldn't get out and play and meet the puppies from the other litters. All we could do was bark at each other. There were dogs from all over, so I learned to speak lots of bark languages. There wasn't much else to do."

On days when it didn't rain, Priscilla would be out in the yard playing with Winston. Sometimes she would throw toys for Winston to fetch. Once in a while, she would quietly creep up close to the fence and yell "Boo!" very loudly. And sometimes the little girl would throw her ball at the fence to try to scare the dogs. Sadly, Priscilla and Winston were *not* good neighbors.

One day, as that rainy summer was coming to an end, Priscilla had fixed her whole tea party set on the table in the middle of the patio. She had to use the patio because the rain had been so bad this season that the yard was soaked, and she didn't want to get any mud on her dress or on Winston's fluffy white fur. She brought out her teddy bear and rag doll and even gave Winston a chair to sit in at the tea table. She was busy pouring pretend tea for her overstuffed guests when her father came to the back door. "Priscilla, I have to run an errand. Your mother is still at work, so there will be no one home. That means you have to come with me. It will be only for a few minutes, but you will have to come along," he told her.

"Oh, no, Daddy, I want to stay home. I'm having tea here with my friends, and if I leave, the tea will be cold before I get back. Please let me stay home, Daddy, please," she pleaded. Winston started barking his little-dog bark as if to say he wanted to stay home, too. Her father sighed.

"Well, Priscilla, I suppose it will be okay. You're old enough now, and I won't be long. Just remember all the rules."

"Okay, Daddy," she said as she turned her attention back to the tea party and promptly forgot all about the rules and her promise to remember them.

On the other side of the fence, the dogs were out enjoying the sunshine. Liberty and Nashota had decided to play tug-o-war with the long rope Sergeant Jeremy had given them. They were pulling and growling and having a good time. It had rained the last three days, and it felt good to Hannah and Spuds just to lie in the grass and let the sun warm them. Spuds, always on guard, was listening to the conversation next door. "That Priscilla is such a whiner," he growled.

"Yes, she doesn't act her age, that's for sure," agreed Hannah. "I'll be glad when school starts again, and she isn't home being a whiney bully all the time."

Nashota and Liberty stopped pulling the rope only for a moment to agree with Spuds and Hannah. "Why does she play with teddy bears? She should play a real game, like tug-o-war. It's so much fun getting dirty!" laughed Liberty.

"No it isn't!" Nashota quickly disagreed. "I just play pull-rope because I want to get strong enough to win someday!"

Chapter Four

"**A**hhh," thought Hannah. "This is just how I wanted to spend my days. The sun is warm, there's a nice, light breeze for the butterflies, and I can hear the river from here as it babbles along over the rocks. It's so relaxing. This is the perfect lazy afternoon." She looked around at the other dogs. They had come through so much together. Now they were all napping happily in the sweet, green grass with full tummies. Spuds was resting in his favorite shady spot with one eye open to keep track of everything. The younger girls had curled up together amid their pile of ropes, bones, and toys, and drifted off to sleep. Hannah curled up on a nice, sunny patch of grass and began an afternoon snooze.

And then they heard it. "Help!" It seemed soft and distant. The noise of the water rushing down the river was nearly loud enough to drown out that little voice. "Help!" There it was again! Nashota and Liberty were so sound asleep after their long play session, that they didn't hear anything. But Spuds opened his other eye. He looked around but didn't see anything to explain the sound. He decided it must have been a dream, closed that eye again, and went back to his nap.

"Help!" Hannah's ears twitched. "Help!" Hannah opened her eyes but didn't see anything. Just as she was about to go back to her nap, she heard it again. "Help!" She sat up. Straining to listen, she perked up her ears. "Help, somebody, help!" There was no doubt now.

She nudged Spuds. "Wake up, I hear someone calling for help. Listen," Hannah whispered.

There was no sound. "Hannah, don't you think we've rescued enough humans in our lifetimes?" Spuds groaned. "There's no one calling for . . . "

"Help! Please, someone help me!" Now it was clear. There was a definite cry for help. Spuds had to admit that it was true this time. He heard it too. But where did it come from? It was hard to tell, being surrounded by the tall fence. It could be coming from anywhere. Then Hannah realized what was happening. It was Priscilla. It had to be. That was her voice, the same little voice that had poked fun at the dogs for weeks. Yes, it was the same little voice coming from the same little bully. She must have ignored the rules her father repeated to her before he left a little earlier. Now something bad had happened, and she was calling for help.

It was hard to convince herself that the dogs should help, but deep inside, Hannah knew it was the right thing to do. Even though Priscilla was not a nice person, Hannah didn't want to be a bad neighbor like Priscilla and ignore the call. She would find a way to help somehow,

but how? They were inside the fence. There was no way out. They had to think of something in a hurry, because Priscilla might be in serious danger. "I wonder where that little Winston is?" Hannah thought. "Why isn't *he* helping Priscilla?"

Then, in a flash, she knew what to do. "Spuds!" she yelled. "Remember that weak spot in the fence? We have to break through there. You have the strength in your jaws to break off the part that's cracked. You have to do it! Right now!"

"Oh, no," Spuds answered. "Sarge worked too hard to get this fence for us. He put it here so he could adopt us all. It's here to protect us, and he trusts us to stay inside. If we break out, Sarge will be sad and maybe mad and the dogcatcher will take us again. And then we may never get another home." Spuds was not at all happy with the idea of breaking out.

Liberty and Nashota agreed with Spuds. "That's right Hannah. They'll take us away, and we might never see each other again," they cried.

"Now listen to me, all of you." Hannah sounded determined. "If something bad happens to Priscilla when we could have saved her, it would be just awful. Sergeant Jeremy will understand that we broke out for a good reason. He knows it's important to do the right thing. After all, he saved us, even though some people didn't care at all about what happened to us, right? If he was here, he would help."

"Well, maybe you're right," Spuds reluctantly agreed. "Okay, I'll break off that part of the fence. But it still won't give us enough space to wiggle through."

Liberty had a great idea. "I'm strongest, Hannah. You said so yourself. I can dig like a mole," she proclaimed. "You break off the fence board, Spuds, and then I'll dig in the dirt under it to make more space. That should work."

"Great idea!" Hannah said. "Now hurry!"

All the pit bulls ran to the weak board in the fence and hooted and hollered to encourage Spuds, as he grabbed the board at the bottom and began to pull and twist with his strong jaws. He was growling while he pulled with all his might. Soon they could hear cracking noises. Then Spuds tumbled backwards as the fence board finally gave way. Liberty leaped into action and started digging as fast as she could. Dirt was flying everywhere, and her two front paws became a blur making a hole deep enough under the fence for everyone to get through. She knew she was doing this for a good cause, and it reminded her of all the times she had dug in dirt just for fun. It helped, too, that the ground was soft from all the rain. It made the job go quickly.

"Yes, you did it!" Nashota yelled, as she was first to wiggle through the escape passageway. She heard the call for help again and followed the sound to the riverbank. Her eyes widened, and she gasped as she saw Priscilla. In a flash, Hannah, Spuds, and Liberty were standing next to Nashota. They were all very worried when they looked over the edge. There was Priscilla holding very tightly to some exposed tree roots with one hand, her feet working to stay pressed against some rocks, and her little Winston folded into her free arm. It wouldn't be much longer before she would loose her grip or her footing and tumble into the rushing water below.

Winston started whimpering. Liberty interpreted, "I'm so sorry, really I am. I shouldn't have come over here near the river. It's just that I was having fun playing ball with Priscilla. She threw it over here, and I went to get it, but I was too close and slid over the edge in the mud. She tried to pull me up, but the mud slid, and we both ended up here. What will we do now? Oh, dear, oh dear."

Hannah thought for only a minute, and she came up with a plan. She started barking out orders like a sergeant again. "Nashota, you are fastest and smallest. You can go back through the hole under the fence faster than we can. Get the pull-rope, and bring it here. Hurry! Liberty, talk to Winston and explain how he can work his way back up the side of the river bank by stepping carefully on tree roots and stones. Go down a little way, where it looks a bit more stable. Keep talking to him and encouraging him to come to your voice. Stay focused so he won't get scared. He's little, so he won't start the mud sliding if he works his way toward you. Go! Now!"

Liberty hurried up river a short distance and started calling to Winston in his bark language. "You can do it, Winston. Watch your step, and move slowly. Hannah will get Priscilla out; don't look back," Liberty encouraged. "That's it, keep coming this way."

Nashota was back in a flash with the rope. "Great!" said Hannah. "Now that Winston is climbing up to Liberty, Priscilla can use both hands to hold the rope and we can pull her up off the side of this river! Spuds, grab hold of the end and help me pull!" Hannah dropped one end of the dogs' big tug-o-war rope over the edge of the river bank. It just barely reached Priscilla, but she knew what to do. She grabbed the end tightly with both hands and pushed up with her feet. She could feel the dirt give way beneath her, as one of her shoes fell off, skipping down the river bank and splashing into the water below. Spuds and Hannah were pulling with all their strength to get Priscilla up and out of danger. Nashota started barking loudly to encourage her not to look down at the river and to keep working her way up the bank. By now, Winston had scrambled up onto solid ground, and he and Liberty joined Nashota. They looked carefully over the edge and barked encouragement to her. When she saw Winston was safe, she was so happy that the last little bit of shimmying up the river bank wasn't hard to do at all.

Meanwhile, it was getting dark out, and Sergeant Jeremy had just arrived home. He thought it was strange that the pets who had rescued him and that he then rescued didn't come bounding to meet him, barking with excitement that evening like they always did. He decided to take a look around out in the back yard. Things seemed oddly quiet as he stepped out onto the lawn. Then he heard loud barking coming from the other side of the fence. That's when he saw it—the hole in the fence and the escape route dug underneath. His heart sank as he imagined the dogs in some terrible trouble. Since he couldn't jump over the fence or fit through the hole his dogs made, he hurried into the house and back out the front door. Running as fast as he could, he followed the sound of all the barking right up to the river

edge of the neighbor's back yard. Arriving just as Priscilla was trying to throw her legs over the edge of the river bank, he joined in the rescue and helped hoist her up onto solid ground. They all lay panting and crying on the ground, tired but happy to be safe again.

Priscilla stood up and realized that her pretty dress was all smeared with the mud. Her hair was dirty and wet, and the curls were gone. Her little dog's fluffy white fur coat was now brown and all stuck down. At first she gasped at the sight, then she started to laugh. Everyone started laughing (and barking) at how funny Priscilla and Winston looked. Then Priscilla went to Spuds, Hannah, Liberty, and Nashota and hugged them one by one. She walked up to

Sergeant Jeremy and thanked him, too. "Mr. Sergeant, I was really, really scared. If it weren't for your pit bulls, I think I might have been in really bad trouble," she said. And then she added, "I don't think your dogs are so scary, or dumb, or lazy. I think they are very nice."

By now, Priscilla's mom and dad had arrived home. They came running out to see what had happened. Her dad started yelling at the sergeant. "What are you and those terrible mean dogs of yours doing in my yard near my child? I'm calling the dogcatcher right now. Priscilla, get in the house and take a bath—immediately!" he screamed.

Priscilla's face crumpled up, and she started to cry. Sergeant Jeremy's head dropped, and his smile went away. Spuds, Hannah, Liberty, and Nashota hung their heads, too. All the joy and laughter stopped as they turned to go home. Then there was a tiny voice. It was Priscilla's. "No, Daddy," she whispered.

"Young lady, do as you were told," her dad growled.

Then a little louder, it came again. "No, Daddy. These dogs are my friends."

Both her parents gasped in astonishment! "Pit bulls can't be friends," they announced. "And neither can any soldier who owns them."

"Oh, yes, Daddy." She felt stronger now. Nashota and Liberty stopped walking away and looked at Priscilla, surprised at what they were hearing. Then Spuds and Hannah paused and turned. "Daddy, they saved Winston and me from falling all the way down into the river. I like them. I like Mr. Sergeant, too. He helped save me, too."

Priscilla's dad looked at Sergeant Jeremy. "Is this true?" he bellowed.

The sergeant looked at Priscilla and her parents. "Yes, it's true. She tried to rescue her little dog and slipped over the edge where the ground is all muddy from the rain. My dogs heard her calling for help and broke through the fence to rescue them both. I got here only at the end to help Priscilla over the edge and back onto safe ground." Jeremy spoke softly, then turned to leave. "Come on dogs," he said to Spuds, Hannah, Liberty, and Nashota. "Come on, let's go home. I have to fix that hole you made in the fence." They all started to plod away.

"Wait," came the dad's voice. "Please wait." He said again. "I owe you my thanks. I see now what happened. You and those four pit bulls saved my little girl's life, and probably her dog's, too. I can't thank you enough. The dogs are heroes. I won't call the dogcatcher. I'll call the

mayor! They should get an award!" Then he looked at Priscilla. "Young lady, you were told about staying away from the river. Now you know why. Will I ever have to tell you that again?" he asked her. He was much calmer now, but he was still angry with Priscilla.

Priscilla looked at her dad and mom, then at her very dirty dog. She slowly shook her head. "No, Daddy, I get it now. I'm sorry." She looked at the sergeant and his pit bulls as they turned to head home. "Thank you," she yelled to them. "Thank you, and I'm sorry."

Her dad called out, "Me, too. I'm sorry, too."

Sergeant Jeremy gave them a salute, and he and his dogs turned to walk home. Spuds walked with a little prance in his step. Then Nashota stopped suddenly and looked back at the river. She took off running back to the edge. Jeremy hollered to her, and then he realized what she was doing. She came strutting back dragging that beautiful pull rope she now loved as much as Liberty did. They arrived home one very happy but tired pack of pit bulls.

As they meandered, exhausted, up the driveway, Jeremy stopped. He called the dogs to him. "Come here guys," he said. Hannah and Spuds slowed down and looked at each other; Liberty and Nashota froze. They were worried about why Jeremy was stopping everyone before they got to the door. All the dogs turned and looked at Jeremy and slowly walked toward him. "Come here, all of you," he said softly. He didn't sound mad, but the dogs weren't sure. Jeremy's face looked different. It didn't have that no-nonsense, army-through-and-through look. In fact, it looked like he might have a tear in his eye. "No, not Sarge," thought Spuds. "He's too tough. What could be upsetting him this much?"

Then Jeremy knelt down and reached out to all his dogs. He hugged them all, and with a cracking voice he said, "I love all you guys. You're the best friends I could ever ask for. No, you're more like my family. You did a good thing today. You're all terrific, and I really love you."

All the dogs sat as still as statues. No one had said that to them before. Most of their lives they'd just been yelled at and told to go away. They could hardly believe it. Hannah moved closer to Jeremy. She sat down next to him and put one paw on his knee. Looking into his eyes, she let out one little bark. Jeremy knew. He knew it meant that they loved him back and loved being his family. Then four happy tails followed Jeremy into the house where they picked out a good dog movie and settled in for the evening.

Chapter Five

"Oh, my gosh, we are going to be late!" exclaimed Sergeant Jeremy. Giving all four dogs baths on the same day was not something he had ever tried to do before. Except for Hannah, those dogs did not like bath time, especially Nashota, who hated to get wet. But today was special. It was Saturday morning, and he and all four dogs were expected at City Hall. Priscilla's mom and dad really *had* called the mayor and told him all about the rescue at the river's edge. The mayor declared this day to be Good Dog Day. He wanted to present the key to the city and a big plaque of honor to the sergeant and his dogs for the good deed they had done.

There would be lots of people at the ceremony, including TV reporters and newspaper photographers. Then they were going to ride down Main Street in a convertible and wave to the people. After that, they would be treated to a great dinner at the mayor's mansion. He had promised big new bones for each of the heroic pit bulls. But now they had to hurry to get there on time.

As they pulled up in front of city hall, Priscilla and her parents were there waiting. So was Mr. Peevish. He was wearing an unusual hat that the dogs had never seen before. Sergeant Jeremy recognized it, though. He knew it meant that Mr. Peevish had been in the service many years earlier.

"Take a look at that!" gasped Liberty. "It's that Mr. Peevish who was always calling the dogcatcher on us!"

"Oh, no," groaned Nashota, "We need to get out of here now!"

"Whoa, hold up girls," said Hannah. "Do you see who is holding his hand?" she asked.

"Hey, it's Priscilla! What do you think that's about?" questioned Spuds.

"Come with me, Grandpa," said Priscilla as she tugged Mr. Peevish's hand. "You are going to meet the bravest dogs in the whole country and the bravest soldier, too. He rescued them, just like they rescued me!"

Well, the mayor said lots of nice things, and everyone applauded when he presented the four dogs and the sergeant with their awards. There were lots of pictures taken, some with just the dogs, some with the sergeant and the dogs, some with the dogs and Priscilla, and some with the dogs and all the people. It seemed to go on forever. Finally, they all walked out of

City Hall, where Sergeant Jeremy and his four brave pit bulls climbed into the waiting convertible for the drive to the mayor's mansion. Nashota looked at the driver and then she looked again. She gasped. "Look everyone, it's the dogcatcher!"

"Oh, no!" barked Spuds. "It's a trick. He's taking us back to the pound!"

Liberty started to whine and whimper. "I want to go back to the sergeant's house. I love having a home."

Hannah jumped up and took a good look at the driver just as he turned and winked at her. She knew those kind eyes. She knew right away he wasn't taking them anywhere but to the party. "It's okay, everyone. He likes us, and he's not taking us back. I'm sure of it. We are all going to the mayor's mansion for the feast!" Then she winked back at the dogcatcher.

People were lined up along Main Street waving and throwing confetti. Sergeant Jeremy was waving back to all the people, and the dogs barked "hello" and "thank you" as the car moved along slowly so everyone could see the heroes. Standing at the side of the street, were Mr. Peevish, Priscilla, and her parents. Sergeant Jeremy was surprised to see Mr. Peevish there, but even more surprised when Mr. Peevish raised his hand and saluted. Sergeant Jeremy snapped back an Army salute and then smiled. So much had happened since his return from the army. He was so glad that he had been able to make a difference for four wonderful

dogs, so they could make a difference for so many others. He kept smiling all evening long at the dinner with the mayor and all the other important people from their town. He smiled for all the cameras, but most of all, he smiled for all the good things he had seen and been a part of. At last, the day was ending. "Won't you stay a little longer, Sergeant?" pleaded the mayor.

"No, thank you, Mr. Mayor. I would love to, but I have four tired heroes to get home," he said. "Besides, I need to get started early tomorrow, if I'm going to get the fence repaired."

And that he did. The next morning Sergeant Jeremy was up even before the dogs. He gathered his tools and wood and nails and hinges, and he headed for the hole in the fence. Why the hinges, you ask? Why, how else can you build a gate?

In the ideal world, every house would have a pit bull, and every pit bull would have a loving home.

Callen
(and the dogs)

Made in the USA
Lexington, KY
03 June 2013